Part I

On either side the river lie
Long fields of barley and of rye,
That clothe the wold and meet the sky;
And thro' the field the road runs by
    To many-tower'd Camelot;
And up and down the people go,
Gazing where the lilies blow
Round an island there below,
    The island of Shalott.

Willows whiten, aspens quiver,
Little breezes dusk and shiver
Thro' the wave that runs for ever
By the island in the river
    Flowing down to Camelot.
Four gray walls, and four gray towers,
Overlook a space of flowers,
And the silent isle imbowers
    The Lady of Shalott.

The Lady of Shalott

Alfred, Lord Tennyson
Illustrated by Charles Keeping

OXFORD
UNIVERSITY PRESS

OXFORD
UNIVERSITY PRESS

Great Clarendon Street, Oxford OX2 6DP

Oxford University Press is a department of the University of Oxford.
It furthers the University's objective of excellence in research,
scholarship, and education by publishing worldwide in

Oxford   New York

Auckland Cape Town Dar es Salaam Hong Kong Karachi
Kuala Lumpur Madrid Melbourne Mexico City Nairobi
New Delhi Shanghai Taipei Toronto

With offices in

Argentina Austria Brazil Chile Czech Republic France Greece
Guatemala Hungary Italy Japan Poland Portugal Singapore
South Korea Switzerland Thailand Turkey Ukraine Vietnam

Oxford is a registered trade mark of Oxford University Press
in the UK and in certain other countries

Illustrations © Charles Keeping 1986

The moral rights of the illustrator have been asserted

Database right Oxford University Press (maker)

First published in 1986
This edition first published in 2013

British Library Cataloguing in Publication Data
Data available

ISBN: 978-0-19-279443-7 (paperback)
10 9 8 7 6 5 4 3 2

Printed in China

Paper used in the production of this book is a natural,
recyclable product made from wood grown in sustainable forests.
The manufacturing process conforms to the environmental
regulations of the country of origin.

By the margin, willow-veil'd,
Slide the heavy barges trail'd
By slow horses; and unhail'd
The shallop flitteth silken-sail'd
      Skimming down to Camelot:
But who hath seen her wave her hand?
Or at the casement seen her stand?
Or is she known in all the land,
      The Lady of Shalott?

Only reapers, reaping early
In among the bearded barley,
Hear a song that echoes cheerly
From the river winding clearly,
    Down to tower'd Camelot:
And by the moon the reaper weary,
Piling sheaves in uplands airy,
Listening, whispers ''Tis the fairy
    Lady of Shalott.'

Part II

There she weaves by night and day
A magic web with colours gay.
She has heard a whisper say,
A curse is on her if she stay
    To look down to Camelot.
She knows not what the curse may be,
And so she weaveth steadily,
And little other care hath she,
    The Lady of Shalott.

And moving thro' a mirror clear
That hangs before her all the year,
Shadows of the world appear.
There she sees the highway near
    Winding down to Camelot:
There the river eddy whirls,
And there the surly village-churls,
And the red cloaks of market girls,
    Pass onward from Shalott.

Sometimes a troop of damsels glad,
An abbot on an ambling pad,
Sometimes a curly shepherd-lad,
Or long-hair'd page in crimson clad,
    Goes by to tower'd Camelot;
And sometimes thro' the mirror blue
The knights come riding two and two:
She hath no loyal knight and true,
    The Lady of Shalott.

But in her web she still delights
To weave the mirror's magic sights,
For often thro' the silent nights
A funeral, with plumes and lights,
    And music, went to Camelot:
Or when the moon was overhead,
Came two young lovers lately wed;
'I am half sick of shadows,' said
    The Lady of Shalott.

Part III

A bow-shot from her bower-eaves,
He rode between the barley-sheaves,
The sun came dazzling thro' the leaves,
And flamed upon the brazen greaves
    Of bold Sir Lancelot.
A red-cross knight for ever kneel'd
To a lady in his shield,
That sparkled on the yellow field,
    Beside remote Shalott.

The gemmy bridle glitter'd free,
Like to some branch of stars we see
Hung in the golden Galaxy.
The bridle bells rang merrily
    As he rode down to Camelot:
And from his blazon'd baldric slung
A mighty silver bugle hung,
And as he rode his armour rung,
    Beside remote Shalott.

All in the blue unclouded weather
Thick-jewell'd shone the saddle-leather,
The helmet and the helmet-feather
Burn'd like one burning flame together,
    As he rode down to Camelot.
As often thro' the purple night,
Below the starry clusters bright,
Some bearded meteor, trailing light,
    Moves over still Shalott.

His broad clear brow in sunlight glow'd;
On burnish'd hooves his war-horse trode;
From underneath his helmet flow'd
His coal-black curls as on he rode,
 As he rode down to Camelot.
From the bank and from the river
He flash'd into the crystal mirror,
'Tirra lirra,' by the river
 Sang Sir Lancelot.

She left the web, she left the loom,
She made three paces thro' the room,
She saw the water-lily bloom,
She saw the helmet and the plume,
    She look'd down to Camelot.
Out flew the web and floated wide;
The mirror crack'd from side to side;
'The curse is come upon me!' cried
    The Lady of Shalott.

Part IV

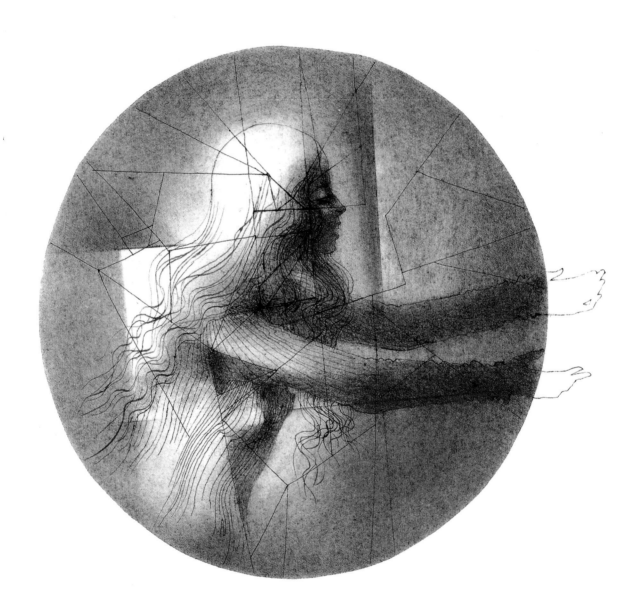

In the stormy east-wind straining,
The pale yellow woods were waning,
The broad stream in his banks complaining,
Heavily the low sky raining
    Over tower'd Camelot;
Down she came and found a boat
Beneath a willow left afloat,
And round about the prow she wrote
    The Lady of Shalott.

And down the river's dim expanse—
Like some bold seer in a trance,
Seeing all his own mischance—
With a glassy countenance
    Did she look to Camelot.
And at the closing of the day
She loosed the chain, and down she lay;
The broad stream bore her far away,
    The Lady of Shalott.

Lying, robed in snowy white
That loosely flew to left and right—
The leaves upon her falling light—
Thro' the noises of the night
    She floated down to Camelot:
And as the boat-head wound along
The willowy hills and fields among,
They heard her singing her last song,
    The Lady of Shalott.

Heard a carol, mournful, holy,
Chanted loudly, chanted lowly,
Till her blood was frozen slowly,
And her eyes were darken'd wholly,
 Turn'd to tower'd Camelot;
For ere she reach'd upon the tide
The first house by the water-side,
Singing in her song she died,
 The Lady of Shalott.

Under tower and balcony,
By garden-wall and gallery,
A gleaming shape she floated by,
Dead-pale between the houses high,
 Silent into Camelot.
Out upon the wharfs they came,
Knight and burgher, lord and dame,
And round the prow they read her name,
 The Lady of Shalott.

Who is this? and what is here?
And in the lighted palace near
Died the sound of royal cheer;
And they cross'd themselves for fear,
　　All the knights at Camelot:
But Lancelot mused a little space;
He said, 'She has a lovely face;
God in His mercy lend her grace,
　　The Lady of Shalott.'